W9-CPL-074

JENNIE'S HAT

JENNIE'S

by EZRA JACK KEATS

PUFFIN BOOKS

HAT

PUFFIN BOOKS
Published by the Penguin Group
Penguin Putnam Books for Young Readers,
345 Hudson Street, New York, New York 10014, U.S.A.
Penguin Books Ltd, 80 Strand, London WC2R ORL, England
Penguin Books Australia Ltd, 250 Camberwell Road, Camberwell, Victoria 3124, Australia
Penguin Books Canada Ltd, 10 Alcorn Avenue, Toronto, Ontario, Canada M4V 3B2
Penguin Books (N.Z.) Ltd, 182-190 Wairau Road, Auckland 10, New Zealand

Penguin Books Ltd, Registered Offices: Harmondsworth, Middlesex, England

First published in the United States of America by Harper & Row, 1966
Published simultaneously by Viking and Puffin Books,
divisions of Penguin Putnam Books for Young Readers, 2003

20

Copyright © Ezra Jack Keats, 1966
Copyright renewed Martin Pope, 1994
All rights reserved

LIBRARY OF CONGRESS CATALOGING-IN-PUBLICATION DATA
Keats, Ezra Jack.
Jennie's hat / by Ezra Jack Keats.
p. cm.
Summary: When the hat Jennie receives from her aunt is not as fancy as
she had hoped, her bird friends decorate it for her.
ISBN 978-0-670-03625-7 (hardcover)—ISBN 978-0-14-250035-4 (pbk.)
[1. Hats—Fiction. 2. Birds—Fiction.] I. Title.
PZ7.K2253 Je 2003 [E]—dc21 2002011316

Manufactured in China

For Debbie Hautzig

A new hat!
Jennie's favorite aunt
promised to send her one as a present.
Jennie waited,
and dreamed,
and waited.
Shutting her eyes, she sighed,
"It'll be big,
and flowery,
and oh—
so very beautiful."

At last it came.

She ran to her room and opened the box.
"Oh, no!" she gasped.
"It's such a *plain* hat!"
"Why, dear, I really think it's quite nice,"
her mother said kindly.
Jennie blinked back her tears
and put the hat under her bed.

She put on a straw basket
to see what sort of hat it would make.
Then she drew pictures.
"HAT-CHOO!" she sneezed.
"Bless you, dear," called her mother,
"and what are you doing?"
"I'm drawing a hat-erpillar—
I mean a caterpillar," answered Jennie.
"Oh, dear," sighed her mother. "I see."

Then she tried on a lampshade,   and a little flower pot,

a TV antenna,

and a shiny pan.
But none of these would do,
not really!

Jennie noticed that it was three o'clock.
Time to feed the birds!
She ran to the cupboard,
filled a paper bag with bread crumbs,
and started for the park.
The birds expected her,
for every Saturday afternoon she went
to the very same spot
to scatter the crumbs.

And birds came!

All sorts of birds,

fluttering

and twittering

and cooing.

They all knew Jennie.

Some ate out of her hand.

Others hopped happily on her head.

Soon every last crumb was gone,

and away they flew!

For a while Jennie forgot about her new hat.

But walking home, Jennie remembered, and wished out loud. "Oh, I wish my new hat were just a little fancier."

The next morning Jennie got up early
and peeped out the window.
What lovely hats she saw!

Later, she went to church
with her father, mother, and friends.
All around her hats appeared
like flowers in a garden.

As they left the church
Jennie saw some birds . . .
Then more and more birds.
Were they following her?

They fluttered down to her plain hat,
carrying red and violet flowers,
and leaves,
colored eggs,
and a paper fan.

They added
a picture of swans on a quiet lake
and some big red and yellow roses.

And two big green and orange leaves,
more pictures,
and some paper flowers,

more real flowers,
and a pink valentine.

Then
all the birds swooped down together,
flapping and fluttering around Jennie's new hat.

Suddenly they all flew away.

On Jennie's head sat the *most* beautiful hat.

At the very top was a nest of chirping young birds!

Jennie felt like chirping too.

Happy from head to toe,

she felt she was walking on air.

People stared in wonder.

Behind her flew the birds,

watchful and proud.

When they all reached her house,
the birds, twittering and singing,
picked up the nest of little ones
and flew back to their home in the park.
Jennie waved good-bye.
"Thank you!" she called.

Jennie's mother helped her wrap the wonderful hat,
piled high with lovely things.
Even after the flowers and leaves had dried,
it would be saved and looked at and remembered
for a long, long time.